M

PATRICK LANE

TORONTO
Exile Editions
1992 1999

IN MEMORY OF
MY FATHER
RED LANE

This edition is published by Exile Editions Limited,
20 Dale Avenue, Toronto, Ontario, Canada   M4W 1K4

SALES DISTRIBUTION:
McArthur & Company
c/o Harper Collins
1995 Markham Road
Toronto, ON
M1B 5M8
toll free:
800 387 0117
800 668 5788 (fax)

The Canada Council
Conseil des Arts du Canada

The publisher wishes to acknowledge
the assistance toward publication of the Canada Council
and the Ontario Arts Council.

ISBN 1-55096-541-7

TABLE OF CONTENTS

"This I have done with my life, and am content.
I wish I could tell you how it is in that dark,
standing in the huge singing and the alien world."

JACK GILBERT
Don Giovanni On His Way To Hell

Part One

HERON

It was the opening into the night
the heron sailed through, holding
with his neck the wind curled in an arch
I wanted, the cause of my stillness

still unknown. What songs I sing
I return to you. Heron song. Blood.
You who cried that you were masters,
here is the particular, the terrible sky.

WOODSHED

The shed is shattered by light, tight streams
finding the holes nails have left,
turning light into a brightness made more beautiful
by dust and the fragile drifting threads
of some spider who wandered through the air
leaving behind it the intricate details of all
its deaths. It is a place where an isolated man
spends hours alone with the winter's wood,
splitting the rounds of fir into fragments, until
in a broken moment he hurls his axe at the wall
only to retrieve it, cursing the opening he's made
as if the rare violence of his life
is a weakness come out of himself, like blood is
when it's made from his own hand, stupid and useless,
the kind of blood he knew as a child when
the dull, crazed silence of his own hands
tore a wall to pieces because it was morning
and there was nothing else to do but destroy.

The child he remembers stands
in the centre of a shed, imagining
each beam of light a fragile sword.
They want to push through the wall of his narrow chest.
He knows if a single beam should touch his skin
it will burn a hole right through him, so he dances
in a slow moving motion shaping his brown body
to fit what little darkness there is, the bright
swords passing through the emptiness he makes of himself
until all there is are fragments of his flesh
left hanging in the air, a far-off hand, a foot,

a single hair, a closed eye that sees what nothing is
and, changed forever by the sight of blood,
waits for the light to find his sight
and burn through his fragile skin a song
whose beat is the heart.

It is a child's lost dream, an art made beautiful
by the waste of time, the boredom, the kind of wish
a child is when his life is the centre of summer
and the whole world heat and waiting.
No longer breathing, his body becomes a spider
who has dragged its past through itself
leaving nothing behind but its future, a wavering
language which if followed leads back to its beginning,
some knot where its web began, some scar whose first
grey word if only understood could explain everything.

It is a child's dream who has found all there is of shadow
and who waits for a single beam of light to make him
whole, or a spider, who when an axe strikes a wall
drags from its body a meaning for the man
then flings itself forever into air,
and swings, a pendulum only a single breath could stop.

SWIFT CURRENT

The day beyond the window moves and drifts
away from us. The poplars far below give themselves
to fall, their tired leaves moving like hands
in the troubled wind. The woman I love also moves,
her face a wet stone in a field
as she lifts her father's legs into the bed.
She leaves then to get more ice for the water
he tries to drink. Her father
weighs only a few pounds, though his hands
are huge, still hold the shape that moved
machines into the earth, the oil rigs
and the combines of the west. His wife sits
beside the bed, the mother of my woman.

The two old people bicker
methodically, their words a kind of music
full of a long complaint
as if the instruments their lives have been
had all the strings stretched wrong.

My eyes are watching the leaves of the poplar
drift across the window. They are trying to find the earth.
Somewhere my woman reaches for ice. I am not with her
though she moves inside my mind,
her face looking down into the cold,
her slender, delicate hands shaking. She
remembers his voice, his face
a formlessness which does not speak
though she imagines his mouth open, his tongue moving

in a place far from her. The man on the bed is trying
to die. He has not eaten now for months
and his body is only bones, the skin stretched
over them so tightly it is translucent, the only
darkness the thick lead of his veins
and beneath them the arteries heaving with all
that is left of his heart's hard breathing.

How tired things are, the poplar trees, the steady
awkwardness of these two voices as they fight
their way to the end of his hours.
The argument of their lives has gone on
for half a century. My woman returns.
I watch her as she fills his cup with ice and holds it
to his lips, his shaking, her tears.

Her mother stares.
She is made out of memory, the hours and days
and years. I imagine
the night she made with him
my woman, holding in her arms that body
broken on a bed. What they have made
touches her father's face,
her gift, holding it for a brief moment
the way a tree holds the wind,
in its shaking leaves all she knows of love.

THE WAR

Those were the last nights of the war, your arms
in their soft circle and the fire beyond us
holding the desert light as I strained to the flames.
It was a time of dust, the time of a child
when he lifts to his mother like a moth out of dry blue,
his body moving the way water moves when it is a cloud
and cannot fall.
                    My father was coming home.
His face had always been a photograph I'd had
to imagine alive, wanting it so, believing love
was what I did not know. I was alive in your arms
as a child who is alone, listening
to the many songs that were from your father, far Virginia
and Kentucky, Old Black Joe, and of a river
deep and slow which was your flesh when it was held
as you were holding me.
                        I don't know what to do
with memory. Somewhere a house was burning,
I remember that, the flames still lift inside me,
and somewhere the woman who was you was crying
with a child inside her arms. This is the flaw of poetry
which cannot heal a woman's face or still a child
who was too young to understand such grief.

I never saw you cry again.
Not when your first child died
with his brain full of the blood of his awkward youth,
or the man who was my father. He died too.

It was a night of dust and flame, a burning house,
your songs, the years of war a man remembers
when he dreams himself awake
and lies in the words of a river, his body
wanting only to be moth, a name, two wings
in search of flame, such words
as were your silence, a child gone into dream,
your eyes alone then watching the last fire die.

DOMINION DAY DANCE

The night is summer
and the hour is heavy with air that moves
like a slow moth in the leaves of the chestnut,
the branches of the elms.
A boy dances in their shadows.
Across the street in The Legion Hall
music falls upon the dancers.
As the boy moves he imagines
a girl whose breasts
are small perfect pains on her chest
and he wants to touch them.
He has sworn tonight to dance
with a girl who is beautiful.
He does not know his desire
to never be alone again
is the beginning of loneliness.
It is a new kind of fear.
It has entered him like a cage enters
an animal, this thing his body does
moving in awkward grace
with nothing in its arms.

THE CHEATING HEART

Bright darkness coming, the sister of my friend
singing Hank Williams, loneliness and the night
when crickets break inside their wings for love.
That mad crying everywhere. The ruin
that was my friend's home, the city begun
among hills that were a wilderness to me.
How when you are young tragedy is always taken
wrong, getting it that way, laughing because
I was young, understanding nothing.
How I saw his sister across the bonfire,
her white face laughing, the shadows beyond.
My friend for the last time beside me.
The unspeakable beauty of our bodies
singing in our flesh long before manhood made us
ashamed. How I loved him. Summer and betrayal.
The crickets in their madness. The cheating heart.
The sister singing far from the fire alone
whom I went to also singing. And returned with,
the fire finally coals, the potatoes we threw in
bursting, the white flesh exploding
that I would not know again, living as I do
far from childhood, her song in the night
the way I turned from him to her white breasts,
the fire blazing.

THE FAR FIELD

We drove for more than an hour, my father's hands
on the truck's wheel, taking us farther and farther
into the hills, both of us watching
the sagebrush and spare pines drift
past, both of us silent. He did not know
what to do with me. I think he thought of
my death, as a man will whose son has chosen
to destroy. I think that's why he drove
so long, afraid to stop for fear
of what he'd do. My mother had cried
when we left, her hands over her mouth,
saying through her splayed fingers
my father's name, speaking
that word as if it were a question. I
sat there peaceful with him,
knowing for these hours he was wholly mine.

He stripped me naked in the last hour of day
and made me stand with my back to him, my bare
feet in the dust, my back and buttocks to him,
a naked boy, hands braced upon the hood,
staring across the metal at the hills.

I remember the limb of the tree falling
upon me, the sound of the white wood crying
as it hurt the air, and the flesh of my body
rising to him as I fell to the ground and rose
only to fall again. I don't remember pain,
remember only what a body feels

when it is beaten, the way it resists
and fails, and the sound of my flesh.

I rose a last time, my father dropping
the limb of the tree beside me.
I stood there in my bones wanting it not to be
over, wanting what had happened to continue, to go
on and on forever, my father's hands on me.

It was as if to be broken was love, as if
the beating was a kind of holding, a man
lifting a child in his huge hands and throwing him
high in the air, the child's wild laughter
as he fell a question spoken into both their lives,
the blood they shared pounding in their chests.

THE KILLER

I have spent too many of my years in you,
have sat inside your body in the bars
while you drank your solitary beers,
their wet circles somehow making sense to me,
the way they almost touched each other
as you lifted the glass to your lips
and drank. I have risen with you
and gone to your truck where the Winchester
rested in its rack and driven through
the country, down the dusty roads,
past the creeks and willows
where grouse and pheasants find their lives
in the quiet thickets. I have stopped
with you and waited for nothing.
I have stepped from that truck
and stood in the gravel, have reached down
for the stone and picked it up and hurled it
at nothing. I have gotten back into the truck
and driven into town past the many friends
and enemies and stopped. I have taken
the rifle from its rack and aimed it
through the window and pressed the trigger,
felt that soft blow in the shoulder
as the rifle recoiled.
                    I have travelled through
the air, through a window, through a wall,
and through my father's chest into his heart, and
I have stayed, a small thing lodged there,
and felt the blood that made me

heave into silence. I have spent most of my life
with you, you whose name I do not know,
you who drove away, leaving
my body inside that heart
lifting up the many pieces, unable
to put any of them together, surrounded
by my father's blood, and wanting
not to be there, wanting only
to be with you, riding quietly
into whatever it was you knew.

FATHER

My father with his bright burst heart, the bullet
exploding in him like some gift the wind had given him,
fell from the sky he'd climbed to, the blood
rushing into him from his startled flesh
so that I imagine his heart a broken sail,
the center suddenly torn and the strong wind rushing
through him, his blood taking him nowhere
at last, his body a whole vessel.

Who will I be,
I who am now as old as his death,
I who have never been a father to my own
lost children, who have left them
to shift in their worlds, their faces shining
in the bewilderment of their lives?

I have turned in my flesh,
rising to the night and the light of the candles
and stood among shadows that are only the stunned
wandering of moths, their burning wings thin sails
in the flickering light. It is here in the shadows
I try to imagine myself young again, a man
who can lift his father from the sky,
take him down and hold him in my arms,
hold him against my mouth,
and with one free hand, stroke his wet red hair
away from his forehead and tell him it is all
right, that I have him, that the bullet
that streamed through the air toward him
was only the wind.

It did not want his death,
was only a bit of wind in the wrong place
tearing him apart. I want then the whole sails of his heart
beating against my chest. I want him smiling
up at me and saying something I can hear at last
instead of this silence, the sound of his voice,
my own children far away rocking in their lives,
his body next to mine, both of us still alive
and not falling, not falling,
the hurt heart dead at last.

FATHERS AND SONS

I will walk across the long slow grass
where the desert sun waits among the stones
and reach down into the heavy earth
and lift your body back into the day.
My hands will swim down through the clay
like white fish who wander in the pools
of underground caves and they will find you
where you lie in the century of your sleep.

My arms will be as huge as the roots of trees,
my shoulders leaves, my hands as delicate
as the wings of fish in white water.
When I find you I will lift you out
into the sun and hold you
the way a son must who is now
as old as you were when you died.
I will lift you in my arms and bear you back.

My breath will blow away the earth
from your eyes and my lips will touch
your lips. They will say the years have been
long. They will speak into your flesh
the word *love* over and over,
as if it was the first word of the whole
earth. I will dance with you and you
will be as a small child asleep in my arms
as I say to the sun, *bless this man who died.*

I will hold you then, your hurt mouth curled
into my chest, and take your lost flesh
into me, make of you myself, and when you are
bone of my bone, and blood of my blood,
I will walk you into the hills and sit
alone with you and neither of us
will be ashamed. My hand and your hand.

I will take those two hands and hold them
together, palm against palm, and lift them
and say, *this is praise, this is the holding
that is father and son.* This I promise you
as I wanted to have promised in the days
of our silence, the nights of our sleeping.

Wait for me. I am coming across the grass
and through the stones. The eyes
of the animals and birds are upon me.
I am walking with my strength.
See, I am almost there.
If you listen you can hear me.
My mouth is open and I am singing.

MOTHER

So many fragile hands. They open, they stir,
the leaves quickening like the bones of birds.
It has been a long time since I was young.
The wind searches among the leaves
and your face returns, a shape that swells in the mouth
until it becomes a single sound, a strange happiness
mostly pain. The poem of you will never be written.
Each time I try to create you I fall into intricate lies,
a place of vague light, uncertain brooding.

I want to remember your breasts. I want to remember
your hands upon me like branches, heavy and swollen,
so they burst inside my mind with leaves
and final flowers that will live until
I forget them. What is it about the wind?
The first small leaves shake
as if they were diseased, as if their ecstasy
demanded shriving, a world of green blood.
It is spring and I am torn by memory.

The lilies-of-the-valley are planted, and pansies,
and the hanging lobelia. Beans thrust out of earth
showing their shoulders to the sun. I see you bent
among lilies and lilacs, laying in your bedding plants.
The sun crosses above your red bandana and the warm
sweat on your face. The years I watched you.
The hands you held me with spent their hours
in the earth.

                    I return to wind.
Your name is a hollow bone, the fragile skull
a bird is after song, the wind on dry sand,
the leaves, your hand. This poem goes nowhere
like a tree whose leaves are stripped by worms.
The wind blows, the branches move,
inconsequential, fragile and forgiven.

SHE

I have no god but you. Inside
your dress, your dry breasts
lie flat against your chest. They are
the first full moons of my earliest night. Inside you
I heard the great drum of your womb
beating and beating its slow measure,
as my hands like the small buds of the jacaranda
reached through the living air for
the murmur of your flesh.

I have no god but you. The immaculate
moment slips away into all the things that are
last. I see you everywhere. You are the old
faces on buses, the women with their eyes
fixed on a place beyond tears. You are
the women who stand beneath willows
on the far side of the river, who lie in the many
cramped rooms, all of your bodies beyond
tides and darkness.

I have no god but you. I fear
the words that mean nothing, the words
that are the cries of the son, the words
a woman calls birth and bereavement,
crying out as a whole body swam out of you
my hands moving like silver salmon
into the pure pale air.

I have no god. But you?
When you gather yourself into silence
and the women chant as they prepare you
for your death, and the men have fallen
to their knees with their last gifts,
will you find me among the strangers
and bring my hands to your breasts?
Will you sing the last song,
the one that begins with the word *yes?*
Will you ask me if I've travelled far?
Or will you say: *I don't know this one.*
What is his name?

THE HAPPY LITTLE TOWNS

Walking the muddy road past the swamp
I thought the butterflies a gift I couldn't bear
there in the sun pulling light into their wings,
drinking sweet water with their tongues.
I was so young I thought I was a man
and that little town a place where a life could be
made, that things like bears or ravens
or the body of a woman were sufficient to themselves
and without guile. That the man walking beside me
had a boot full of blood was nothing more
than the end of a day. A man who had opened
his body with an axe. It could have easily been
a boy with an eye scooped out, or a woman
bleeding into diapers for a month, afraid
to tell her man she'd lost his child.

That was the year my wife slept with my best friend.
I could tell her now the summer was oblivion,
that the blood gone from a body cannot be
given back, the wound opening like a mouth
without forgiveness. The inside of the body
when it first feels air feels only noise, as the
butterfly when it first crawls out of itself
feels only wonder and never eats again. I remember
the brightness of the days as my hands healed
the many injuries, the hours alone. It wasn't sadness
or self-pity, only oblivion, the kind a boy feels
when he is made into a man, wanting only to be
held, for the first time in his life without love.

The wreckage of that world stayed wreckage, though
we tried to build it back. The steady years of trying,
her taking the flowers I picked in the fields
and placing them in a jar where we watched them die.
What I remember most is that injured man who,
with the dignity of the very poor, told me he was
sorry to bother me, as if his wound could have waited
for a better time to happen; my hands putting him
back together, the stitches climbing up his leg
like small black insects I created out of nothing,
the curved steel needle entering his pale flesh,
pulling behind it a thread thin as a butterfly's
tongue, him saying he was sorry, and me knowing
for the first time in my life what that must mean.

BROTHERS

We were brothers long before we were men,
small, tough because the days kept hurting us,
days when a word like *beauty* had to be learned,
our mother making us spell it over and over
until it seemed the word lost meaning
and was only punishment. It was before I had glasses.
I didn't know I was almost blind, and didn't know
what I saw I didn't see. Years later, looking
at Van Gogh's wonderful cypress tree,
that blue pain twisting like a heart into the stars,
I saw my original world, everything out of focus
and understood that even small birds die and mountains
burn when a child wants them to. Whenever I smell
fresh bread I remember us climbing out the window
at dawn and running across the alley in our pyjamas
to steal bread from the bakery, that warm yeast
lifting us from sleep as it cooled in the last air.

Sometimes when I'm afraid I walk into the hills
where the trees are. Stunted desert pines
the world leaves alive because they're useless.
The earth is made of terrible stones and sand.
There is no rain. *Sustain* our mother might have said
and we would spell it together, our voices
singing. I remember how it took a day to reach you
riding the miles north into your madness, thinking
you were dead. It was like listening to a song
from the war and suddenly knowing there were men

who stumbled into death singing it, desert men
who didn't believe their eyes, the sudden silence
in that strange country the end of their lives.

It's why a pine tree in the hills can heal me,
why when I hold you in my arms after singing
the old songs, I begin to understand how words are made,
the awkward letters at the beginning of *beauty*,
the way sound closes inside the word *sustain*,
the rain that only deserts know, living things
in a place they are far from, or two children
standing in the dust, their mouths breaking open
the hot white heart, leaving behind them
the crusts of bread for birds.

Part Two

THE BIRTH OF NARRATIVE

The boy's father killing the cat in the garage,
swinging the two-by-four through the air,
the cat leaping, trying to escape,
and the boy's seventeen-year-old wife standing there
pregnant, crying, telling him to stop, and the father,
having begun all of it and now somehow trapped,
starting to cry too, still swinging that board,
the cat leaping, the boy somewhere else working,
pulling, I think, green lumber off a chain,
waiting until he could come home to the story.

WET COTTON

She was lying on the bed, her skirt lifted
up over her breasts and face. He could hear her breathing
in the quiet room, a sound that made him think of cotton
when it has been wet for a long time. She was
sleeping, the drugs and alcohol heavy inside her.
Something white hung from her naked foot.

She didn't belong to anybody.

The boy watched as his older brother
pushed the large sausage into her.
He pulled it out very slowly
and then,
because what he had done had become a bond among them,
he made each man take a bite from it,
some of them retching, some of them not.

But what he is remembering is not that.
It was their leaning forward after the laughter,
how
as they watched his brother push the sausage in, they had become
thin, their faces shining, narrow and white
in the soft deflected light from the hall.

Their faces thin,
and her on the bed breathing like wet cotton.

PRECISION

The party was almost over. One of the guests, an older man no one knew who had lost the wig that had curled over his eyes, danced naked in the largest room. His body was strange, the legs too short and his torso too long as if he had wanted to stay a child and refused to grow. The women encouraged him, laughing at the grey pubic hair, his lank penis and his arms as he staggered before them, his face slack and featureless. When he finally fell two women pulled him to the door and rolled him outside. It was one of the last hours. Someone would fight soon. Someone in a moment would stumble in from outside, his cheek torn, the flesh hanging in a flap from his chin. A woman would wrap a pillowcase around his face and leave him to bleed in the bathtub. The men in the basement would begin arguing about who got the only pistol and who had to make do with knives. Soon the ones who had to leave would go, but not quite yet. First the argument had to start, the fight over the girl with red hair, how to split up what was left. The boy in the corner who would be a writer someday watched everything very closely, the way the woman on the couch breathed, her dark skirt pulled up over her face, the fabric lifting very gently from where her mouth had to be, the way blood mixed with water in the tub, the laughing, the arguments, women screaming, men sullen and cold, staring through their whiskey at nothing, the hour moving through its difficulties, the boy not knowing yet, but waiting for something he would later describe when he was much older, his green eyes moving across a hand as it turned into a fist, a dark breast hanging from a torn blouse, a man with only one shoe, someone vomiting, something about to happen in the next hour that would, for the boy in the corner, resolve the immense complexity of this night.

THE ATTITUDE OF MOURNING

He had walked out of the Pitti Palace into the rain, thinking
of that painting of Franz Hals' high in the corner
where the light was dimmest, its anonymity intact.
The one of the young girl in the attitude of mourning.
She had reminded him of the vulture he had seen
in South America years ago, the one that huddled
under the geraniums during the rain,
not blinking, its two dark wings
pegged through the cardinal joints to the ground
while everything above it flowered red.
The rain striking its naked head.
But that was years ago when he was young.
Back then he had thought he understood
the magnitude of such an exile.

But this was not Medellin, it was
Florence with all its clarity intact,
its opulence a kind of tired memory, malignant
as light when it struggles with the rain
in the winter of Italy. It is the same
light an apple contains that rots from the inside,
that slow umber growing from the center
toward the beauty the skin inhabits.

That is what art is, he thought, the perversity
of wanting that, the choosing of innocence
as a model for loss. He imagined the stained hands
of Franz Hals, their sureness as they removed

the young girl's shift, the light
from the northern window, the girl's mother
at the door counting the money
the canvas ready, the brush and the other brushes.

Later that night the palace was what he had wanted,
the walls rotting, the frescoes crumbling. The woman there
was all flesh, someone who simply wanted less.
This century would never paint her.
He looked at her breasts and her long wrists
and understood that pleasure when it becomes cruelty
is inward, a kind of bruise the body grows,
and knew then
he wasn't speaking of her but of himself.

Do you want me to hurt you? he asked.
Nò, she said, *non c'e necessita,*
her dialect peculiar, so that the host,
the large Englishman with the bare red feet
who had been talking of his mother and her distaste,
how she had told him when he was still a boy
she had slept with his father
only once, unsuccessfully, told me I should ignore her.
She is from Rome, he said. *And they know nothing in Rome.*

GRIEF

He sat at the foot of the low bed and watched her cry.
It was not like Rome burning and it was not
like the spare fires he had built
when he was alone in the wilderness,
the ones he sat away from, the ones he put out
when he was tired of watching.
Her grief was of another kind, an event
that was merely ornament, a thing
that perishes as it is made, as a performance
in a northern town perishes line by line
with no one to remember it, something less than art
as time is less than merit. He had made her love him.

She hadn't wanted to. He had shaped her love
by shaping himself, giving himself to her
in the exactness of her integrity, becoming
her, and so, becoming less, their time
together an intimacy which was only imitation.
Sitting there he felt the same
as when he was a child and dressed
in his mother's clothes, his posturing
in front of her mirror, the inaccuracy
of that kind of dance.

He understood his gluttony, the wanting more,
his greed for her loss, the pain
she seemed to love more than him.

She did not tell him to go away, and
she did not call out to him.
What he had was what an observer has,
the man who gazes alone from a private box
protected by velvet curtains, a glass of good wine beside him,
the play going on and him with no rights, one way
or another, the man who watches with detachment
as a critic does, having no stake in the event.

PRIVACIES

She was the lover of his friend, a girl
with red hair and a body Renoir might have painted,
small and opulent, a figure Renoir would have placed
to the side as a decoration of the larger event, two men
talking perhaps about art while the woman lay on the lawn,
naked, waiting for something to happen.

That night when his friend was teaching
he had made love to her
and after, she asked him not to tell, as if betrayal
were made easier with promises. *He is
taking me away to Montreal,* she said. Later
when his friend came home
they had all sat together on the bed and drunk wine,
her watching as his friend and he laughed at the bad poems
of their enemies, his friend's last year at the university,
Montreal, and beyond that Jerusalem. Earlier his friend
had told him he would not take her with him.

He watched her touching his friend, her lover,
her small hand resting lightly on his shoulder, the look
in her eyes which his friend mistook for love.
Her artful modesty. His friend's indifference.
He thought of them later when they would be alone
together, their privacy, the touching.
For a moment, in the middle of their lives,
he was strangely happy with his burden.

BREAD

He sat in the rich woman's house.
She was no longer beautiful, and
perhaps she had never been beautiful
but had only listened to the mirrors
in the briefest of hours: that finger, this breast,
a single perfect pearl, a sound,
someone leaving, a bit of dust on the floor.

And he sat there among the vases of flowers
happy to be in such a place, far
from the busy street, happy to have
a glass of good wine, and to be with a woman
who was no longer
beautiful.
                    Suddenly,
he wanted to share with her something
he had, but there was nothing
except the piece of bread he had saved
from breakfast, a bit of bread
he had meant to give to the birds
at twilight, but was night now
and he had forgotten them.
Look at what I have found,
he said, *look at the bread.*

She smiled: *I know, I know,* she said.
*Everyone has gone to the country.
I think I am the only one left.*

THE BOOK OF KNOWLEDGE

He had been reading volume seven of The Book Of Knowledge
and he got to thinking about those fakirs,
the difference between one nail and a thousand,
so he had taken his mother's sewing basket
and slowly, with what he thought then was patience,
took her needles and shaking only a little,
pushed them slowly through the skin
of his left arm, in and then out, the nine needles
resting there in a row, the flesh white and hard.
There was very little blood.
He pulled his sleeve over them
and went down to breakfast, his father quiet
as he drank his coffee, his sister watchful,
his brothers arguing over the last bits of meat.
Each time he lifted his fork
he could feel the fabric of his sleeve
catch at the needles, his flesh moving.
Sitting there he realized for the first time
how dangerous he was.

FRAGILITY

She came from Normandy, one of those
villages on the lower Seine
where they make the good Calvados, the kind
you can only find there. She was very small.
He remembers that, the bones of her feet
fragile in his hands. They met
in Cuzco, the city of cut stone,
and parted in the Cartagena before
the tourists came, the one where,
if you closed your eyes and smelled it
you could remember Drake and his plundering,
his queen and glory. She had red hair
and that fair clear skin you can see through
at night in the last of the candles.

THE FIREBREATHER

(in memory: Marcel Horne)

She took him to the shed in the field behind the house.
For six days he had sat there naked in the darkness without food
while the water he was allowed went slowly bad
in the New Mexico heat. On the last day the gypsy woman
came in and told him she was tired of his impatience.
She began to talk of her day, the morning in the market,
her husband's drinking, her daughter's whoring
after a Mexican businessman who sold melons in Texas.
While she spoke she began to light wooden matches,
striking them on a flat stone she held on her lap.
She sat very close to him and as each match flared
she would hold it to his skin, sticking it there,
the match burning, the smell of his own flesh.
He looked at his arms and chest, the way
the match would sometimes burn all the way
to the end and not fall off, the match curling,
those black stems sticking from him like fragile quills.
This went on for a long time until he no longer remembered
what he was there for, the sweat from his face and shoulders
running down his body, that sweet salt touching his wounds.
Then she opened his mouth, burning his tongue and lips.
The pain you feel is the pain of the outward, she said.
Later I will teach you the other pain.
When you have learned that you will be ready
to breathe fire.

BALANCE

He watched the horses come, huge in the afternoon,
their rubber hooves a dull sound under the screaming,
the riders swinging clubs to the right and left.
As he watched he saw a woman with a child go down
under a black horse, the horse careful not to step on her
as the rider leaned like a polo player
and struck her across the shoulders as she fell.
The horse and rider looked like they had practised this
a long time, the rider balanced perfectly,
the horse moving as if without effort, though
he could see the great muscles moving under its skin,
the crowd splintering into the many
narrow streets that led from the Avenida del Sol.
He had always remembered that, the horse's gentleness,
so strange in a body that large, the rider's steady grace,
and the woman
rising after they passed over, the look on her face,
the baby crying, the street almost empty, people
stepping from doorways to sit at the tables again,
the waiters bringing wine and beer.

STYLITES

Most of the women had gone to bed, some of them alone
and some of them with the men they had chosen
or the women. He was very drunk and very happy
and he had not wanted anyone.
The woman his friend had travelled there for
had taken a soldier instead, saying, he likes
to dress up in my clothes. When she had gone
and only a few men were left drinking
he climbed up to where his friend was
among the beams and rafters
high above the floor. His friend
didn't know how he had got there.
He was afraid of heights.
They had sat there together
looking out at the far night,
the drunken voices of the last men below
rising to them on the clear cool air,
taking a drink, taking another one.
They talked quietly about the food
he would need, the ropes
he had to have to tie himself with
in order to sleep, how long
he intended to stay there, the night,
and the many nights to come.

DETAIL

The room was thirty inches by thirty inches
and there was a light in a small wire cage
in the ceiling above him.
He could stand but he could not sit
and after a week his legs began to swell.
The wood of the narrow door was a pale yellow.
It was a kind of wood he'd never seen before.
There was almost no grain, the thin striations
on the narrow boards almost invisible,
varying only slightly. He spent his hours
tracing the patterns, following them
the same way the saw had followed the wood
into the heart of the tree, cutting
a little deeper each time. He knew
he would tell this story years later
and when he did this would be the place
where his listeners would shake their heads,
understanding the attention to such detail,
his legs swelling, the light,
and the thin cage of wire
he kept trying but couldn't reach.

LA SCALA

Ready to go to her then, saying he was sorry
to himself and almost believing it, saying it again
as if it were a song a baritone sings
during an opera in a provincial town
while the tenor and soprano watch from the wings
just before entering for the finale, the moment
just after the tragedy, and always during the third
or fourth performance when all the singers
are at last sure of the version
they have settled for, the reviews in,
the songs always in another language
which is never translated and
which the singers had to memorize,
their precise imitation making it
another kind of beauty, and going to her
singing it, singing it.

ESTIMATES

She was driving, the dark Ontario night
sliding past them, the dying elms, the maples
heavy with fall. In the back seat, his friend,
the blond woman who had been very sad
for a long time, was listening to them talk.
The driver, a beautiful woman who was also famous,
told him that most of her lovers had been impotent.
How big is your cock? she asked him.
He thought about it for a moment and then
he told her. She was quiet
and he could hear his friend
breathing in the back seat.
He told the woman it was something that men do,
measure themselves. Why, he said,
he didn't know. She said, *I've never had*
one that big inside me. He was listening to her
but he was also thinking. *I'm sorry,* he said
I lied.
Oh, she said.
And his friend, the blond woman who was very sad,
said nothing, her breath steady and slow, listening
as the conversation went on, something
about parrots, something about drugs in Miami,
her friend who had been a mule, another
friend who had killed somebody
somewhere.

Did you ever kill anybody? the woman who was driving asked.

IMPRESSION

Imagine a man who remembers. Imagine
a man who has left his country forever, a man
his friends helped over the mountains say, or over
the northern deserts, a man who his friends knew
would be arrested, tortured, made to tell all
his secrets. Imagine this man years later
remembering her, thinking of their nights
together, the smell of her flesh
on his hands, her dark hair
above him, her back arching, the way
her breasts would rise, shuddering
as small golden fish do when they lift
their bodies into the sun.
She is the one he is remembering now,
the one they caught three days later.
Imagine him thinking of her, remembering,
his mind going around and around, her breasts,
the corner of that last street he saw,
the blind man who sold pineapple there,
the one people used to stand and watch,
the sharpness of his knife, the way
he would cut the pineapples perfectly,
each slice precisely the same as the last,
the one who never hurt himself,
seeing that in his mind, the van, the noise,
him on the floor under the rags and papers,
shaking, going somewhere,
the mountains say, or the desert.

VOYEUR

If she were lying naked and a little drunk
on a narrow mattress in a rented room
and the man she had just made love to
was sitting by the window talking to her husband,
his best friend, who had called out of the blue,
and all the lights in the city went suddenly out,
what would she think about as she listened
to the man's voice, the long pauses,
the occasional quiet laughter? Would she
hold her hands up and try to see them?
Would she touch her shoulders,
crossing her long arms across her breasts?
Or would she do nothing, nothing at all
in the darkness surrounding her?

DESIRE

She was a tall woman, very beautiful, the kind
whose legs seem to travel forever, limber and long, as if
they had spent their whole
lives wandering, sure of the many directions.
But it was not her legs.
It was the three dark hairs that grew from her breast.
She would lie there, very still, and he
would lean down as if from a great distance,
not touching her anywhere,
and with his teeth pull them from her flesh,
the breast lifting
and then
falling back slowly, settling into its shape,
curved and heavy
down and across her long ribs. One, and then
another. What he loved was
not being able to see her face, imagining it,
the strain as he pulled
very slowly,
her nipple tightening, the brown skin growing
toward his lips.

THE IMAGE

Now that he was older
the artists had begun to paint him, and the photographers,
the clever ones with their miniature machines came
and arranged him in gardens and poolrooms, bars and verandas,
to capture the images of who he was, who they thought
he had been. Most of the artists were his age
but some were younger, beautiful young men,
and women with large hands, their hair pulled back
tight, their clothes unruly. He liked them the best.
He liked the way they would walk around him
after spending days and nights with his books,
his poems, the way they would stop and stare
while they painted him, all his words in their minds,
all the suffering intact, precise and imaginable.

NOTATION

He has found a piece of paper on his desk.
On it is written the following:
"277 – male version of life"
"287 – nature, with her utter lack of sentiment..."
He is looking at the words
and for a moment, for just a brief moment,
not very long, a few seconds perhaps,
he feels the room around him,
its strangeness,
the way what little light there is
will not reach into the corners.

SHORT STORY

And then there was Billy, the quiet kid from Salmon Arm, Jesus, everybody liked Billy, who loved her so badly. He kept saying it: *I love her, God, I love her*, over coffee at The Coldwater Hotel, her in the bar, the baby crying. She was Nicola Indian, long gone down that road, and then Billy, after the strike and no money, the months of standing through the long winter of '56 while trucks and scabs rolled by, the RCMP young and tough, from places like Hamilton and St. John, went home and sat up all one night and in the morning took the baby by the heels and smashed it against the wall, and Rose, the Indian girl, the wife, came to our house, and said: *That Billy, that Billy*, and had a cup of tea and then went down to the Nicola River and this barely spring, ice still holding in the log jams, took off every stitch of clothes and floated all the way to Spence's Bridge. I think it was Cole Robinson found her, he'd been short-logging there, and when he asked her what the hell she was doing naked in the creek, said nothing, said: *That Billy, that Billy*.

Part Three

THE LAST FARM

On the last farm a man lives out the dream of a man,
his body taking on the shape of an animal
he no longer knows, his face in the corner
where shed-doors meet becoming the sharp
muzzle of a starving fox as it stands inside
its own sweet death. As a woman's isolate body
changes where she stands into a coyote mad with dust,
a badger low to the ground, its grey coat torn,
attacking anything that comes out of the night.

Beyond the wind and dust, images make out of the mind
a man who thinks his woman water, a thin brown sack of skin,
and tries to drink her. He walks into the wind
where he finds a piece of metal he can lift in his hands,
the bullet breaking like a mouth against his eyes.
Or a woman in a cellar thick with dust
searching for seeds among the remembered arms of potatoes,
her hands closing like eyes inside the bins,
or a child in a room above a room, her face
pressed against glass as the world below her collapses
upon itself. She hears a body thrown against a wall,
a rising sound that lifts her into night.

This is a place that has forgotten itself.
It is a place of dust and wind, a sound
that is the sun breathing into sky a color
impossible as flesh. It forgets itself, forgets
what it has seen, the light and dark, the machines,
the people, the many images they thought they were, the father
who was the mother who was the child who was the man,
a woman, a well, the wind, the endless dust.

THE GARDEN

From his window he looks down on the winter garden.
The rocks he carried across a mountain range
and the great plains rest in the arrangement of snow.
Beneath the spare limbs of the forsythia
the Japanese lantern glows in the thin sun, its patina
slowly moving toward the color
which will make it finally beautiful,
something that will occur long after he is dead.

Sitting there he thinks of his wife and wonders
what it is she knows now. He remembers just after
the divorce, her telling him how
she had slept with all of his friends.
Over the years. It was not
a confession, it was a sharing, as if their past
needed that kind of clarity. He hadn't known that, but
he laughed with her anyway. So they had sat there
on the couch in the room he had once inhabited with her,
all the things surrounding him what he would once have
called his belongings. He thinks he remembers his children
playing somewhere in the house but he's not sure.

The sun at the horizon moves and the garden changes,
the shapes under the snow assuming light. He thinks
that he will put a candle in the lantern
so he can watch it at night, the shadows
wavering in the cold, the stones around it

like white animals come to worship something
they have never seen before, a light in the darkness,
their bodies surrounding it in wonder, all of them,
as if they were alive, saying they would never forget it
and believing they were telling themselves
if only for this one night the truth.

THE CHILDREN

The children are singing.
Hear them as they rise out of the deep hollows,
the tangles of wildwood and wandering vines.
They are lifting from the shadows
where the black creek water flows
over mud and stones. They have left behind
the green whip of a snake
thrown like a necklace into the trees,
and the body of a turtle, heavy,
buried beneath stones. The birds
are silent behind them. The paths
are still, waiting for the quiet ones,
the battered red face of the fox,
the thin touch of the raccoon
as she lifts her paws from their hiding.
The children are returning.
You cannot see their faces or their hands,
not yet. There are only their voices
rising from the tangle of vines,
the wet of black water.
Listen. There is nothing
to be afraid of now. Nothing.
The children are singing the old songs,
their hands empty, their small sharp eyes
alive.

THE PATH

(for Phyllis Webb)

A branch intrudes and the tree is lost.
Birds sing in the wreckage
wondering at the plenty that precedes
starvation, the fasting unto death.
It is another giving makes the dance.
It is the hour when to move is more
than moving, a child at first light
on the forest path who stops at song
because she is a child and the night
is gone. The light is not of stars
though she knows the light
and thinks it her. She is the stillness
before song breaks to song. All things
rise like breathing in her mind.
Our sitting in the house is far away.
We see through glass. The dance is not
her dance. She does not move in any way
we can imagine. What we see is light.

THE MAN IN THE ROOM WATCHING TV

Night after night the dog in the fenced run
howls with a spare intent
as the moon goes down. The last snow
rots below the withered apple tree
and on the far streets the heavy
rusted cars of brutal children
trace and retrace their track between
the bridges of this northern city.

In a room in a small blue house
a man masturbates in the flickering light
from a television. On the screen
men act out pleasure with a bleak incompetence.
There is no grace in the woman
who fellates a man on the screen while another
slaps her thick buttocks with his hands.

The man watching them has relinquished virtue,
his boredom rising out of a last regret. He thinks he is
searching for the same kind of clarity Rimbaud had
when he cracked lice between his nails
in Abyssinia, sick and dying, dreaming
of Verlaine. He is the pearl that slowly sloughs its skin
until it becomes the grain of sand. It is a pearl
on a necklace on the throat of a woman dying of syphilis
in a hotel in Paris. There is in the watching man
a steady measure, *accidie,* that word
for which we have no meaning.

It is what the man has. He is a word
without meaning. The look on his face is
a pale surprise, the look in the eyes
of someone just before
they are thrown through a windshield.
That kind of look. That seeing.

AT THE EDGE

At the edge of the sea the trees lean away from the wind
their spare trunks bare where they twist into the sky
above the stones. The great birds cry
as they wheel above the foam, the carrion eagle
heavy with greed, tormenting the gulls,
and the osprey, elegant and alone
as she drops upon a salmon, lifting, lifting
the thrashing weight to her nest on the far cliffs.
Everywhere there are bones.

The woman walks here,
her blue eyes touching upon the rare
unbroken shells, the skeletons thrown up by the heavy tides
to lie in the hot locked pools among the rocks. Crabs
crawl among her feet, their claws raised up
in praise. She has come to the sea to raise
her dead, the child she gave to the waters,
a thing she might have called a daughter had it lived.

The man who holds her in his closed eyes
has gone past loss. He has brought her here to heal
and waits now like a mouth that cannot open. He imagines her
searching in the stones for something greater than
herself, a perfect living thing
that will make her whole again. She knows
he is there and there is nothing she can do.

The sea lifts and falls only to lift again,
a green lung heavy with breathing.
In a moment she will turn around
and he will still be waiting. They are both learning
what the salmon knows when it lifts into the air to hang
from the osprey's wings, what the crows sing
as they search in the wind for flesh.
She will not turn around and he will not open his eyes.
The crabs retreat into the foam, the clamshells close.
Somewhere in a nest on a broken tree the osprey fledglings
wait. A fish flies toward them as the sea, obeying a moon
on the far side of the world, retreats. They are retreating.
This is what they have come to. This place. Here.

THE MEADOW

The day in the meadow when he reached for her
and pulled her down into the wild grass
their cries were animals singing
so that the hawk circling far above them,
hungry, her young like soft explosions
on the nest, flew on, forgetting what she saw.
How they lay there in their limbs
laughing at the world they had begun
not knowing the words that later they would use
when the injuries began,
the betrayals,
the other bodies they would touch
imagining desire was to be cold
and perfectly alone. And then the confessions,
their hands finding each other awkwardly,
promising themselves it would never happen again
and almost believing it
as they said the word *love* over and over,
as if that hawk circling in the sky above their meadow
had stopped and held there above the human
saying to herself
of all things surely these will live.

GIFTS

Who are you? Are you
the one who opened your blouse and gave me
in both your hands your breasts, holding them out to me
while my wife in the dark living room
knelt on the blue carpet?
If you are the one, I remember wanting
not to be with you, but to be
with her, watching while someone's hand
moved in her thick dark hair.
Where have you gone?
What gifts have I refused?
Why do I remember now only the carpet
and the narrow feet of my wife
white against that heavy blue?

DARK BLOOMS

I lie down in nothing but air.
The garden is in this room growing. It is
growing the way a cactus grows whose spines
are no explanation for paradise. Somewhere
in the heart of all of it there is a flower waiting,
its dark bloom a thunder. O but the air.
It holds me in the measure of what distance is,
a place clean as morning. She is coming with her songs.
And I am waiting for her, waiting for her
to begin, my nakedness like the cactus
who dreams among its spines of flowers
everywhere inside me.

THE WOMAN ON HER KNEES

The woman on her knees falls forward
and her breasts fall with her. They are
the shape of the pears on the lean branches
of trees I knew in childhood. I picked them,
held their weight in my hands, knew
there were seeds within the flesh
I would find like the stars I found
in the meadows of my young nights.
Her body spreads above me like a heart.
Holding her shoulders I hold nothing
in my hands, her breasts
above me swaying with memory, the blossoms gone
that were her childhood, her shoulders trembling.
Only my mouth is alive.

THE LOVERS

The man she lies with in the bed
is kneeling before his first lover, his mouth
holding like a stone the head of a cock,
a swollen thing that is still
years away from manhood. His dream
is a cape the body has thrown
over his mind, so much like the vessel
a monk's face is when it is
buried in its folds of curled black cloth.

Inside the man the child he was
suckles on a child, a boy who will go
towards his duty, the regular Sunday beating,
a ritual the man remembers watching,
seeing the black belt rise and fall
upon the boy he would have called a lover
if he'd known the word. In a year that boy would
die, beaten to death by his father.

It is the old story of poverty and song,
the years of bare feet and flesh,
and the long hours of early day, when children
play, inventing worlds they know nothing of.

The woman he lies with holds her thighs together,
trying to imagine what it is
to be only flesh. The man
beside her is far away in the place
he calls a little death, and she is waiting for him
to return. While he is gone

she dreams him in a war, leaving her behind
for the world in which there is nothing but men.
Listen, she says: *If you ever tried to go to a war
I'd break your hands, I'd break your fucking legs.*

Yes, the man says, *yes,* for one moment
staring into a place where a man this woman
has created stands with a rifle. The man she
has made in his mind is about to kill him.
It is just after a child
dies, a child far back in his mind
he thinks he loved. *I love you,* he says, his mouth
taking her breast into his mouth, his hand
moving on her thighs, opening her again, feeling
her flesh give itself to him. It is all
he can do in this place that is many
places. *But there is no war,* he says.
Damn you, she says, *damn you,*
meaning love, meaning nothing but words.

IN THE DARK

In the dark my body glows
where the moonlight from the window, slow and pure,
falls across my legs. I hold myself in my hand,
alone and fallen from the hour. The night moves
gently as the light from the far side
of the world climbs in a soft crescent across
the last sand of Africa and opens to the grey waters
it must cross to find me. On my belly
my seed cools in a pool, the many lives
swimming slower and slower as they move toward a place
where there is no life, the blood gone back to the body.

I try to remember what I imagined
and am strangely ashamed, the woman
in my mind a stranger whose body
existed inside mine and was made up
only of parts, a breast, a thigh, a hand.

Now she is almost asleep, drowsy,
her eyes closed, her mouth partly open,
her chest rising and falling with mine.
I want my seed in her.
I want her to be lying beside me
as my woman lies after love, laughing at her own wonder.

I touch the thousands of lives with my finger
and lift them to my lips. *This is who you are,*
I say. You are the taste of still water.
You are a pool in a forest where frogs sing
as they swim among weeds, where isolate turtles
wait for the sun to heal them, their huge bodies
still, their eyes full of patience as they
stare at the moonlight on the waters. My hand
is a dragonfly hanging from a flower. My eyes
are open. What they see is a darkness all their own.

THE SOUND

The sound that is a man when he dances with men
The dance that precedes laughter and killing,

Their cries spilling like quick water on the air.
The sound that is a woman when she watches

Other women, her throat thick as they walk
With swollen bellies under the dying elms.

It is the dragonfly in the mouth of the cat,
The dream dog running, his long tongue

Moving in grey folds across the floor.
The sound that holds like color in the grass.

It is a claw or a club or a woman
Raising her white ass and pushing it like a heart

As she takes the flesh deep in her belly.
It is a forehead falling on a naked back,

A mouth packed with earth, a face, a fist,
Two bodies when they feel their fingers

Crawl like alien animals on sweet flesh.
It is the voice of a child in the dark

Who reaches out to take the moon in his mouth
and thinks it love, the sound as he wakes up.

HANDS

Your fingernails are the shells of foraging beetles,
your palms a desert, the shape of a gun and a breast,

an intricate map leading nowhere. It is you
who open the legs of women to find the secret

places where pleasure and pain live side by side
like fluttering birds caught in lime.

It is you who delight in the mystery of the knife,
the curves of carved ivory, the pen that writes

over and over the same dark sound of the mind.
You search each other for scars, tracing

the lines that formed deep in your mother's belly,
the closed eggs of your fists growing like wings.

The hieroglyphs she left you with say nothing.
The heart and the head, the fate, the life,

the canyons of skin you lose yourself in. There
is not a part of you you do not know, not

an opening you have not entered. How many times
have you danced? What is the language of signs

you make on the impossible parchment of the air?
What are your names when there is no one there

to name you? What artifacts do you hold in the night
with your long pale fingers, your heavy thumbs?

When you lift yourselves up to my sleeping face
what is it you hold? What stops you?

ORPHEUS

(for Leonard Cohen)

He is mostly laughter and willingly,
thinking of all those years of music
and the tears given to the wind, struggling

back up through all that silence, a second death
a cruelty he began to understand. To flee
from women, knowing only the trees and stones

could hear his song. This was the mystery
men turned to, a giving up to grief,
a going into song without complaint, for what

else but love had brought him here
to this place of birds and serpents? But to see
such death, and for what? To speak at last

in a voice that touched no one, the women
with their rakes and hoes hacking him to death
for whom the trees let fall their leaves?

And then to have his song lie beached on Lesbos
with Bacchus squatting on his head, cacophony and din
and nothing more? But these are only questions.

He should have known love would bring him this,
and of course the greed of women, their desire,
thinking death a suitable revenge upon neglect.

Orpheus who sang man's mysteries and died for it.
You too who dance upon the beach, you who have never
listened, listen now: the leaves fall without you

and the birds who once sang with you sing alone.
Make your lament. It is only noise.
The whole world does not hear you.

EARS

Your curves are the labyrinth the wind makes
with the sea, the sound of ancient women

whispering the secrets that are the defeat of men,
the plaintive agonies that are time and memory.

Without you nothing has a name. Without you the world
returns to silence, the chaos that existed

before thought was born. Sisters,
your dream is the dream of tongues, the word

that forgets itself over and over again.
Nouns lose themselves in your caverns

as verbs twist the grey mass of the mind.
Your whole being waits for a word

that can never be said. A mouth whispers
and the body gives birth to itself, a flesh

made of cancer and leprosy, pestilence and pain.
It makes its way toward the empty towers of churches.

It invents bells. It searches with its tongue
for a woman to enter, a name to utter

so that a god can be born
whose name will be man. The ears listen to the laughter

from the soft beds of the seraglio, the waiting rooms
of the harem. Who is singing? What are her names?

EARS 2

All the strangers are lonely, you
bright simple shells who share the sea,

who listen to the voices of the ancient
men on the corners as they mutter the many

secrets we no longer understand. Like the hands
unborn foetuses hold before they bud with fingers

you swim in the unimaginable water of the air
creating patterns out of cacophony, the chaos

which surrounds me. Such perfect music, elegant
and alone, as a man is who stares with great severity

at the wheeling gulls and folds his clothes
before walking into their cries, the sound

as of the great water when it enters his openings,
that shout of silence. Oh, I have known him!

I have in the long cold nights heard the whisper
and made from the sound of his name, myself.

How strange the hours, the white foam drifting back
in the slow susseration of the sea, the sound of things

as they give themselves back to my dreams,
the night I listen to in my sleeping.

FEET

You are the only safety I know, the secret of journeys,
of wanting and forgetfulness. You are all I know of earth.

Your hard yellow skin finds its own way among broken glass
and stones – shape of the body in sand and snow, you

were the dream inside the drum of my mother's belly.
It was you she traced with her long hands, feeling within

her the shape of my wandering. You swam inside her womb
in the endless salt sea, moving like fins in the quiet waters.

Of all my body you are the most alien and unknowable, your bones
the shape of a cat in the sky, a bird among stones. The right

is small, troubled by night. It follows its brother,
hides behind its other, moves like a snake moves,

delicate and dangerous. The left is always breaking free.
It finds its own way, the path of grief and forgiveness,

happiness and hate. It is you who pulls the body
around corners, you who dances alone, beating the time

of the heart, the head, the breath. When I sleep you find
each other, stumble together awkwardly. You wish for

the delicacy of fingers and lips, a tongue to sing, an eyelid
or an ear. Dumb brutes, made only for earth, when I stand

upon my head and lift you into sky, you are ashamed and naked,
hating your ugliness, the mottled yellow of your soles, the

horny nails, misshapen toes. When my lover takes you into her
mouth what does she sing to you with her teeth and tongue?

When she suckles each toe do you become nipples? When you enter
her do you remember the first sea or the last? Far from me,

are you omega or alpha, dumb beasts, animals
that carry me where I am afraid to go? I know nothing

of your lives. I forget you in the moments of beauty.
You caress each other, tell each other the many stories of roads

and forests, the first story of the sea, the last story of earth.
Wherever you are going tonight, take me with you.

THE WHITE PARROT

(for Brian Brett)

The white parrot is a contradiction, two languages,
Each one a memory that has forgotten itself. It is

The color of a foetus, a beast with wings, the imitation
Of an animal. Its cry is less than a cat, greater than a woman.

Part cactus, part armadillo, its feathers are illusions,
Ancient scales made out of wind and wandering.

When it sinks its tired claws into your shoulder and eats
With its thick black tongue the air, who is with you?

What is the beast you break bread with? What is sleep's name?
Upside down inside your mind it screams, gutteral,

Contemptuous of the cage that bears it. When your body sleeps
What is the name that watches you? Who is perched

On your wrist? What is the word in the mouth of the anti-bird?
What is inside the antique eye that photographs you?

When you arrive at my door the parrot enters first on its claws.
It drags you with it, tethered on a leash around your thumb.

In your cupped hands you carry the offering, the fruits of earth
The seeds that are yet to be born.

Soul-eater, singer from the dead. All it remembers of jungles
Are what you have forgotten. It knows nothing of the sea,

Nothing of the air. Earth-bird. It lives in the cage outside
The cage. Under its heavy wings you will find only men.

PROMISES

I will sit and hold my hours together
saying to the great wound of the dawn

the words: cactus blossom, plum, and reverie
and believe them all the way to the last sun,

my woman curled and sleeping in our bed
giving herself to the dreams of birds and hands

which are of all things most simple,
or the cat bringing back to me a startled wren

letting it go again to see it fly
happy at last with a life it understands.

I do not want to hear again the voice
that is a man who lives in the mountains

so all I can do with his trembling is say yes
when he asks me if I really am his friend

his tongue so drunk it barely moves
as the early morning animals eat his head

or see the cat climb over the picket fence
a dead sparrow in his mouth, the teeth chattering,

the wild clouds huge and falling on the west
and my woman once again too far away.

SO WE COME

We have come to this
with what gifts we have, holding to
the terror we know and trust, the memory of things

we reach for, all our dreams,
the shaking drift of wings across our minds
when we are lost in sleep. There is no image

as we lift out of the dark
drowning, our whole bodies holding us there
in our beds, screaming. As I hold you

rocking you there in the dark, your hair wet
and your eyes staring. The horse that rides your night
rides mine as you slip back to silence,

your body still. This moment
when I want for you what little can be given,
when the night is huge

and a bird in some far tree cries out
because a shadow moved. My hand upon your breast,
the distant sound of breathing

in the street below, the night horse running through us
in the dark we made
giving as we have ourselves to dreams.

HALF-LIFE

There was a time when an exact half-mile was the distance
my body made walking from a door to the edge of town,
the first faint houses crouched in sleep and silence,
their lights a wedge, thin as the night they held,
the distance a body moves when it remembers.
It is as if I am water drawn out of the deep
that feels a loss in its ascendancy, something
left behind in the steady seepage of the well,
the bucket full, rising to the hands that draw it up.

I am a darkness whose direction is away
from things. I have sold the birthright.
I go now into night, imagining
ahead of me one light in a window, radiant.
But whose room glows? Who among the many
rises in what could be laughter after love
or pain that cries out of silence or a fist,
or someone alone, lost in their flesh. One who waits
for some presence to arrive out of the night
and cries in the still moment we call dread.

This monster at the heart I travel towards decays
half-life by half-life as distance does
so that the shining in me, radiant, is a hand-print left
showing the bones beneath the flesh; a radiation,
my body flowing outward on the page, palimpsest,
as if I lift from a carapace my mind has made and see
two wings where once was only sleep.
What is on my mind is half a heart.

Creatures cry, the scrape and whistle of things that know
the night. A snake's quick crawl away from the sound of leaves,
a far dog howling at the world beyond its chains,
a cat's harsh cry who finds in sound its own lost solitude,
the far lights of a car on another road. I count the poles
as I counted them as a boy, hearing voices running through
thin wires, faint and querulous, the distances between.
They cry in the wires like insects
who batter against a yard light left on late,
their bodies flaring as they die upon their wings.

Whose house hides at the end of this half-mile?
Who stares out of the dark at a single window
framed by lilacs and honeysuckle vines?
Who has risen in the night? Did he know
what bodies know when naked and alone he lifted
from sleep to wander among the many silent rooms,
while behind closed doors the others, touched by what
they thought was sound, lie half-asleep,
afraid, no longer sure of where they rest?

DINNER

I would like to have dinner with the man
who didn't follow Christ, the one who,
when Jesus said: *Follow me and I*
will make you fishers of men, decided
to go fishing instead, getting in his boat,
pushing out from shore, his nets clean
and repaired, thinking I will have to work
even harder now in order to feed
everyone left behind. I would like
to sit on the beach with him
in front of a careful fire,
his wife and children asleep,
sharing a glass of wine, both of us
telling stories about what we'd done
with our lives, the ones we caught,
the ones that got away.

Afterword

A number of these poems appeared in earlier versions in the magazines *Border Crossings, Grain, Newest Review,* and *Exile.* I wish to thank the editors for their continued faith. *The Last Farm* was read on the CBC program *Ambience,* with thanks to Wayne Schmalz. Five poems, *Dominion Day Dance, The Cheating Heart, The Happy Little Towns, Hands,* and *Brothers,* orginally appeared in my *Selected Poems* published by Oxford University Press in 1987. They fit here and I thank them for allowing me to reprint them. I especially want to thank my companion, Lorna Crozier, whose critical skill and acumen led to changes in some of these poems. Her grace has kept me alive.

I want to thank *The Canada Council* and *The Ontario Arts Council,* both of whom at different times invested in the time and changes it took to complete this collection. My brother's early death and my father's murder changed my life in the Sixties. It was only recently, twenty-five years later, I felt capable of approaching that time with poetry. *Mortal Remains* is a dark title yet it is somehow appropriate. Poetry cannot save us but it can provide us with some small redemption. As I said in one of the poems:

> *The wind blows, the branches move,*
> *inconsequential, fragile and forgiven.*